Glaciers

Glaciers

Margaret W. Carruthers

Watts LIBRARY™

Franklin Watts
A Division of Scholastic Inc.
New York • Toronto • London • Auckland • Sydney
Mexico City • New Delhi • Hong Kong
Danbury, Connecticut

For Richard

Note to readers: Definitions for words in **bold** can be found in the Glossary at the back of this book.

Photographs © 2005: Alaska Stock Images/Russell Fiord: 10; AP/Wide World Photos: 48 (Michael Probst), 9 (Ivan Sekretarev); Corbis Images: 52 (Argentine Antarctic Institute/Reuters), 37 (Tom Bean), 50 (Morton Beebe), 18 (Ric Ergenbright), 22 (Peter Guttman), 42 (Wolfgang Kaehler), 16 (Matthias Kulka), 14 (Danny Lehman), 38 (William Manning), 28 (David Muench), 6 (NASA/Reuters), 32 (Graham Neden/Ecoscene), 8 (Pat O'Hara), 30, 46, 49 (Galen Rowell), 17 (Phil Schermeister), 25 (Paul A. Souders), 36 (Spaceborne Imaging Radar-C/X-band Synthetic Aperture), 13, 29 (Hubert Stadler), 26 (Kennan Ward), 20 (Stuart Westmorland), cover (Jim Zuckerman), 21 33; Nature Picture Library Ltd./Jeremy Walker: 12; NHPA/B. & C. Alexander: 2, 44.

Illustration by Bob Italiano

The photograph on the cover shows a glacier in Juneau, Alaska. The photograph opposite the title page shows Skaftafell Glacier reflected in a pond at Skaftafell National Park in Iceland.

Library of Congress Cataloging-in-Publication Data

Carruthers, Margaret W.
  Glaciers / by Margaret W. Carruthers.
     p. cm. — (Watts library)
  Includes bibliographical references and index.
  ISBN 0-531-12285-9
  1. Glaciers—Juvenile literature. I. Title. II. Series.
  GB2403.C37 2005
  551.31'2—dc22   2005001464

Contents

The International Space Station, shown here in 2000, helps scientists monitor glaciers on Earth.

Kolka Glacier, Russia

In August 2002, astronauts and cosmonauts aboard the International Space Station focused their camera on Mount Kazbek in the Caucasus Mountains of southern Russia. From their position 250 miles (about 400 kilometers) above Earth's surface, they could clearly see the ice field that covers the mountaintop and the **glaciers** that snake slowly down the valleys.

Scientists are monitoring glaciers such as these because they are interested in

what is happening to them as Earth's climate changes. Many parts of the world are warming up and, as a result, the ice is melting. By comparing images taken at different times, scientists can watch the glaciers transform as they respond to changes in the climate.

Unfortunately, the glaciers on Mount Kazbek reacted much more quickly and dramatically than anyone expected. On September 20, 2002, just one month after the image was taken, the Kolka Glacier collapsed. A chunk of ice fifty stories high broke off the glacier and began sliding down the Karmadon Gorge. Gathering speed, the ice scoured the valley, gathering boulders, rocks, and mud. The thick mixture of ice and rock slid 15 miles (24 km), racing down the valley at speeds of up to 60 miles (about 100 km) per hour.

By the time it was over, the avalanche had buried the tiny village of Karmadon in 20 million tons (18 million metric tons) of ice, rock, and mud. Nearly 150 people were killed.

After Russia's Kolka Glacier collapsed, this mass of ice, rocks and other debris raced down the mountain in Karmadon Gorge.

Word Root

The word *glacier* comes from the word *glace,* which is French for "ice."

Glaciers can be found around the world. The Hubbard Glacier in the Russell Fjord Wilderness Area is in southeastern Alaska.

Chapter One

Seas and Rivers of Ice

Valley glaciers, cirque glaciers, ice sheets, ice shelves, fjord glaciers, ice caps, ice streams, and outlet glaciers are all different varieties of the same thing: a mass of ice that flows—usually slowly—under its own weight. Glaciers can be found on every continent, from the poles to the equator, from sea level to mountaintops. Some, such as the valley glaciers in the Himalayas, flow like rivers down wide mountain valleys. Others, such as the thick, dome-shaped Greenland Ice

What Is a Glacier?

A glacier is any permanent mass of ice that flows, regardless of its size, shape, or location.

Fox Glacier, located in Westland National Park on the western side of New Zealand's South Island, is fed by four other glaciers.

Sheet, spread out over entire continents. Right now, **glacier ice** covers nearly 6 million square miles (about 15 million square km). That's about 10 percent of Earth's land surface.

Some Kinds of Glaciers

Valley glaciers are what most people envision when they think of glaciers. They are a few hundred to a 1,000 feet thick (about 100 to 333 meters thick) and fill long, wide valleys between mountain ridges. Cirque glaciers fill small, bowl-shaped depressions in the high mountains. They are typically about 100 feet (30 m) or more thick. Fjord glaciers are valley glaciers that begin on land but end up in the sea. Their **beds** are below sea level.

Ice sheets are the largest glaciers. Roughly circular or oval, they cover hundreds of thousands to millions of square miles. They almost completely cover the underlying rocks. They can be several miles thick, thickest at the center and thinning out toward the edges. The edge of an ice sheet is sharp and steep.

Ice caps are dome-shaped layers of ice that cover mountaintops. They resemble ice sheets, but they are smaller. Ice streams are zones of fast-moving ice within an ice sheet. Outlet glaciers are valley glaciers connected to larger ice caps or ice sheets. Ice shelves are the parts of an ice sheet that are floating on sea water rather than touching **bedrock.**

Glacier Anatomy

Although each glacier is unique, they all have a few things in common. All glaciers are made of ice, water, air, and **sediment.** They all flow like rivers. Their area grows or shrinks, depending on the weather and climate. And all glaciers have the same basic anatomy.

Accumulation is the addition of ice to a glacier. The **accumulation zone** is the part of a glacier where most of the ice forms, mainly through snowfall. Ablation is the loss of ice from a glacier. The **ablation zone** is the region where the glacier loses the ice. Melting, evaporation, **calving**, wind **erosion**, and avalanching are all forms of ablation. In reality, snow is lost in the accumulation zone, and snow falls in the ablation zone.

Glaciers flow like rivers. A glacial system flows under the pull of gravity.

Subglacial Lakes

There are more than seventy lakes beneath the Antarctic Ice Sheet. The largest is Lake Vostok, which is about 150 miles (about 250 km) long, 30 miles (50 km) wide, and 1,300 feet (400 m) deep. It has been there for at least 500,000 years. Some scientists think it could have been there 40 million years ago!

But over the course of a year, the amount of snow that falls in the accumulation zone is more than the amount that is lost. In the ablation zone, the reverse is true.

It is fairly easy to tell the difference between the accumulation zone and the ablation zone. The accumulation zone is at the highest part of a valley glacier or near the middle of an ice sheet. The ablation zone is at the low end of a valley glacier or

A glacier's edge is called its terminus. This photograph shows the terminus of Mendenhall Glacier near Juneau, Alaska.

the edge of an ice sheet. The accumulation zone is smooth, white, and snow-covered. The ablation zone is rough, dirty, and scarred with streams, pits, drainage holes called **moulins,** and deep cracks called **crevasses.** The boundary between the two zones is called the equilibrium line.

The end of a glacier or the edge of an ice sheet is called the **terminus** (*terminal* means "end"), or nose, margin, or snout. The noses of most valley glaciers are rounded, and some are nearly black with a mixture of boulders, gravel, sand, and mud called **moraine.** The edges of most ice sheets and ice caps, however, are sharp, steep, very clean, and white.

The bottom of the glacier is called its base. The gravel, mud, or solid bedrock it moves over is called the bed. Beneath many glaciers are streams and even lakes. These can form when ice melts on the surface, forming **meltwater,** and then trickles down and collects at the base.

Making a Glacier

In the northeastern and the mountainous western United States, blizzards can dump several feet of snow in one day. This thick layer of snow might stay around for a few months, but it won't become a glacier unless it remains all year long, with more snow piling up year after year. Some snow can melt, but more would have to fall to replace it.

Newly fallen snow is light and airy because between and within the snowflakes is a lot of space. In fact, about 90 percent of a snowflake is just air. After a few days on the ground,

How Cold Is Cold?

The coldest ice known in a glacier is about –22 degrees Fahrenheit (–30 degrees Celsius).

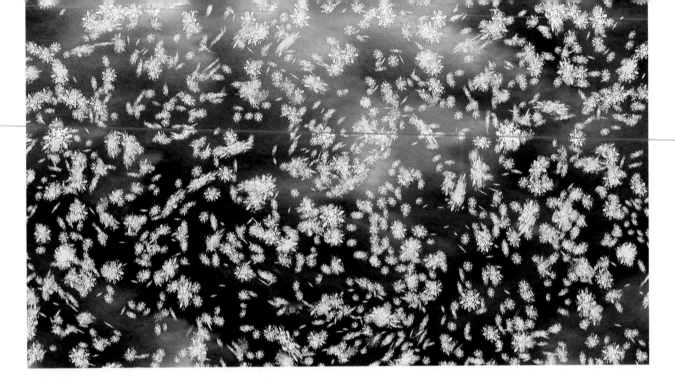

Newly fallen snow is light and airy.

the snowflakes begin to lose their hexagonal shape. The points of the snowflake melt or evaporate. That water then refreezes closer to the center of the flake. Eventually, snowflakes become dense little granules of ice. If they survive for an entire year, these grains are called **firn.**

As the snow piles up, firn grains are pressed closer and closer together, squashed by the weight of the snow above. On some glaciers, water trickles down from above and freezes within the empty space between the grains. The ice gets denser and denser, and the water molecules in the ice rearrange themselves to form larger and larger crystals.

When the layer of ice gets to be about 30 feet (10 m) thick, it can no longer hold its own weight. The ice starts to change shape and flow downhill or out to the sides. It becomes a true glacier.

Growing and Shrinking

Several things can happen to a glacier after it forms. If more ice is added to the glacier than melts, evaporates, or breaks off, the glacier will grow, or **advance.** If there is more ablation than accumulation, the glacier will shrink in area, or **retreat.** If ablation equals accumulation, the glacier will remain stable.

Whether a glacier advances, retreats, or remains stable depends on the weather. Some years it may grow, and other years it may shrink. But what really controls the fate of a glacier is the climate, which is the weather over the long term. Glaciers grow when the climate is cool and wet. They loose mass, or shrink, when it is warmer or dryer.

Since scientists began studying glaciers in the mid-1700s, the climate in most parts of the world has warmed. And since the mid-1800s, nearly every glacier on Earth has retreated. The Agassiz Glacier in Montana's Glacier National Park covers only one-quarter of the area it covered when it was first mapped around 1850. The nose of Qori Kalis outlet glacier in the Andes Mountains of Peru is retreating 500 feet (150 m) every year. The Taku Glacier in Alaska is an exception. Between 1890 and 1989, it advanced more than 4.5 miles (7 km).

The jagged Taku Glacier pushes through a forest toward the Taku River outside of Juneau, Alaska.

17

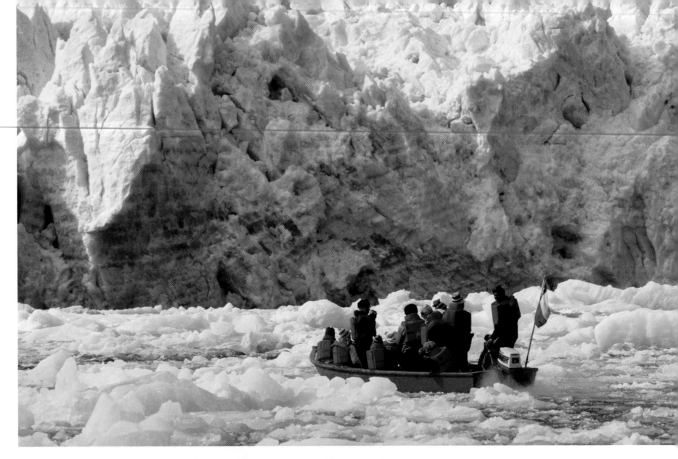

Tourists from a cruise ship approach San Rafael Glacier in a small excursion boat. San Rafael in Chile is one of the world's fastest-moving glaciers.

Flowing and Sliding

The words *advance*, *shrink*, and *retreat* are confusing because they give the impression that the glacier itself is moving forward or pulling backward. Actually, it is the ice that is always moving from the accumulation zone down toward the ablation zone. Even when the glacier is stable or retreating, the ice is moving downslope. You can think of it as a line at the grocery store. The line can get longer or shorter or stay the same length, but the people in the line are always moving toward the cash register.

Glacier ice moves for the same reason that river water moves—gravity. Gravity pulls the ice downhill and makes the thick part of the ice sheet press down so much that it pushes ice out into thinner regions. Glacier ice also flows like river water, only much more slowly. While river water flows many miles per day, most glacier ice only moves a few inches to yards per day. The San Rafael Glacier in Chile is one of the fastest in the world. Parts of it move more than 35 feet (10 m) per day.

If you've ever thrown a bunch of sticks into a river, you've probably noticed that some move downstream faster than others. That's because water in the river flows at different speeds. Just like river water, glacial ice flows at different speeds, depending on where it is in the glacier. Ice near the glacier's base and sides moves more slowly than ice in the middle because it is slowed down by friction with the bedrock.

The exact speed of glacier ice differs from place to place, season to season, and year to year. It depends on the thickness of the ice, the temperature of the ice, and the bed's slope and roughness. Ice moves faster when it is warm, the glacier is thick, the slope is steep, the bed is smooth, and liquid water is present.

Glacier ice moves in two main ways: flowing within the glacier and sliding along the bed. The ice crystals inside a glacier are under a lot of stress. The mass of ice above is pressing down on them, while gravity is pulling them downhill. All this stress makes the ice crystals deform. They form new crystals out of the old ones, and they creep forward. Creeping is a bit strange. When an ice crystal creeps, parts of it slide past other parts. Very slowly, individual ice crystals within a glacier creep downhill.

This water-sculpted iceberg has a blue tint in the sunlight. The floating mass of ice was calved from Alaska's Le Conte Glacier.

Glaciers in relatively warm areas are not frozen to their bases. They have a thin layer of liquid water between their base and their bed. There are two reasons for this. First of all, during the summer in particular, a lot of meltwater can trickle from the surface down through small cracks, crevasses, and moulins, and collect at the base. Second, if the glacier is thick enough, its weight causes the ice at the base to melt. If you press on ice, it melts. This is called pressure melting.

As you might expect, the water at the base of the glacier makes it slippery, allowing it to slide downhill. Glaciologists call this basal sliding. Extremely cold glaciers don't slide very much because they are almost completely frozen to their beds.

Surging

Once in a while, a glacier will move very quickly, or **surge** forward. In 1966, for example, the Steele Glacier in the Yukon of Canada moved 5 miles (8 km) in just a few weeks. In 1993, the Bering Glacier in Alaska surged down its valley 330 feet (100

This photograph from 1966 shows Steele Glacier stretching along a snowcapped Alaskan mountain range.

m) per day. It may not sound fast, but if you live or work in the glacier valley, it could be disastrous.

The main reason glaciers don't move quickly all the time is because of the friction between the glacier's base and its bed. Surges occur when something happens to make the glacier overcome the friction. The stress at the base is just too much, and it begins slipping very quickly. Or maybe the surface of the glacier melts a lot. The meltwater trickles down to the base, making it more slippery than it was before.

Not far from the North Pole is Jakobshavn Glacier in western Greenland.

Chapter Two

From Antarctica to Mount Kenya

There are two places to look for glaciers. They are found at high latitudes—closer to the North and South poles—where it is very cold almost all year long because of the distance from the equator. Glaciers are also found up in the mountains where it's cold because of the high altitude.

Scientists can classify glaciers in different ways. One way is by their size and location. **Continental glaciers,** such as the Greenland and Antarctic ice sheets, are thick layers of ice that cover huge landmasses. **Alpine glaciers,** such as valley glaciers and cirque glaciers, are smaller bodies of ice found among the mountain peaks and ridges. Alpine glaciers are surrounded by rocky mountains. They are confined to the valleys and can move only one way: downhill. Continental glaciers, on the other hand, are so thick that they cover nearly the entire landscape. Without any mountains in the way, they can move in any direction.

Glaciers Galore

There are more than 67,000 glaciers listed on the World Glacier Inventory.

Polar and Temperate Glaciers

Another way to group glaciers is by the climate of their environment. There are two main categories: polar glaciers and temperate glaciers.

As you would expect, polar glaciers are found near the North and South poles. The ice sheets in Antarctica and Greenland, and the ice caps in Iceland and parts of Canada, are all polar glaciers. The North Pole has no glaciers because there is no dry land there. Although glaciers may end in the sea, they form only on land. The ice at the North Pole is frozen ocean water, or sea ice, floating on the Arctic Ocean.

Near the poles, the summertime temperature only briefly goes above the freezing point, or 32° F (0° C). It doesn't snow very much because the polar air is too cold to hold much moisture. But because it is so cold, polar glaciers don't ablate very quickly either. When they do lose mass, it is mostly

through calving, evaporating, and blowing away, rather than melting. This happens only during a brief period of a few weeks during the summer.

Temperate glaciers, on the other hand, are found in **temperate zones,** which are much closer to the equator. Temperate zones have a mild climate, which means not too hot and not too cold. Most of North America is temperate, for example.

Most temperate glaciers are in high mountains where it stays cold and wet enough for snow to build up. There are temperate glaciers in mountains all over the world, including the Southern Alps of New Zealand, the Andes of South America, the Himalayas of Asia, and the Rocky Mountains of North

Closer to the equator are the temperate glaciers of New Zealand's Southern Alps.

A pool of icy water collects liquid from the melting edge of a glacier on Mount Kenya in Kenya, Africa.

America. There are even a few glaciers in the mountains of tropical countries such as Ecuador and Kenya, right on the equator.

The ice in temperate glaciers is at the freezing point—32° F (0° C)—for much of the year. This is because the warm season in the mountains lasts longer than in the polar regions. Though the temperatures are still low, much of the ice is only just cold enough to be frozen. As a result, these glaciers contain a lot of liquid water, which makes them smaller and faster moving than polar glaciers.

Some glaciers have characteristics of both temperate glaciers and polar glaciers. These are known as subpolar glaciers. Parts of the Greenland Ice Sheet and parts of the Antarctic ice sheets are subpolar.

A Look from Above

Let's say someone gave you a satellite image or an air photo of a glacier. Even if you had no idea where on Earth it was located, you would still be able to make an educated guess about its environment. Several clues make it easy to determine quickly whether a particular glacier is temperate or polar.

The first clue is vegetation. No trees or other large plants grow near polar glaciers in places such as Greenland. It's just too cold. Around temperate glaciers in places such as Alaska, on the other hand, there can be dense, lush forests. In fact, the nose of the Franz Josef Glacier in New Zealand is actually in a rain forest.

Another clue is the shape of the glacier terminus. Since polar glaciers lose most of their mass by calving and evaporation, rather than melting, their noses are sharp and steep. The terminus of a temperate glacier, however, is rounded and often dark with sediment from the base and moraine that it has plowed in front.

Snowball Earth Hypothesis

Some scientists think that about 750 million to 600 million years ago, Earth was covered entirely in ice. According to the so-called Snowball Earth hypothesis, a sheet of ice up to 0.6 miles (1 km) thick covered Earth from pole to pole. Most scientists agree that there was a **glacial period,** or **ice age,** at that time. But the evidence that the entire earth was covered in ice is not as clear. Many scientists don't think it happened at all.

A third clue is the color of the water near the glacier. If it is clear, the glacier is polar. If it is milky, powder blue, or muddy, the glacier is temperate. This is because temperate glaciers can slide along the ground much more than polar glaciers, which are essentially frozen to the ground. As temperate glaciers slide, they grind up the rock below. Streams flowing beneath and out from under the glaciers then carry the finely ground sediments called rock flour to the rivers or seas. Polar glaciers don't grind up as much rock, and there aren't many streams to carry the rock to the ocean.

Pederson Glacier in Alaska's Kenai Fjords National Park is a polar glacier.

Icy Chameleons

Like chameleons, glaciers adapt to their environment. Over time, if the climate gets colder, alpine glaciers can grow and merge with one another to form a continental glacier—or a temperate glacier can take on the characteristics of a polar glacier. If it gets warmer, a continental glacier can thin and shrink, becoming a bunch of separate alpine glaciers. A polar glacier can slowly warm up to become more like a temperate glacier.

The village of Ilulissat, also known by its Danish name Jakobshavn, coexists with the Jakobshavn Glacier in Greenland.

A U.S. scientist stands on a high tower to collect ice, snow, and air samples at the South Pole, Antarctica.

Chapter Three

Glaciers from Top to Bottom

Scientists have been studying glaciers for hundreds of years. They have hiked up the tallest mountains to collect samples. They have trekked across the ice sheets to set up weather stations. They have flown airplanes over glaciers and focused satellites on them. They have camped out for months at a time in the cold, thin air far from civilization. Studying glaciers is a lot easier now than it was in the early 1800s, but it is still difficult, dangerous, and expensive.

31

Mapping the Surface

Mapping anything as big as a glacier is a challenging task. In the past, everything had to be done by hand and on foot—or by sea. Ice sheets are so enormous that until recently, large regions of them were never explored. Scientists still use many of the same methods, but now they get a lot of help from satellites and airplanes.

Air photos and satellite images show how much land a glacier covers. Scientists can then use the global positioning system (GPS) of satellites, radio towers, or small receivers to determine the exact locations of particular points on a glacier. Scientists can also use GPS to measure the shape of the surface of a glacier.

Shattered ice sheets descend from the Antarctic Plateau to sea level at the Theron Mountains in Antarctica.

However, a faster way to measure a glacier's shape is to use a laser altimeter mounted on a plane or a satellite. The laser altimeter sends a flash of light down to the glacier. It then calculates the height of a particular point on the glacier by measuring the time it takes for the light to travel down to the glacier and back up again. To map a large area, laser altimeters send and receive thousands of flashes every second.

Lake Pukaki (left) and Lake Tekapo are glacier-fed lakes high in the Southern Alps of New Zealand's South Island. Mount Cook and the Tasman Glacier are in the upper left corner of this computer-generated image.

Clocking a Glacier

In the past, if scientists wanted to measure the speed of the ice in a glacier, they would have to find a distinctive boulder or plant a flag in a certain spot on the glacier and mark its position on a map. Then they would have to come back some time later to survey how far it had moved. Now scientists can do this using GPS. GPS measurements are so exact that it's possible to tell if a flag moved just 0.5 inches (about 1 centimeter). With enough markers and enough time, scientists can create a velocity map of the glacier.

A faster way to clock a glacier is by using a method called satellite radar interferometry. A satellite orbiting high above Earth takes radar pictures of the glacier. It sends radio waves down to the glacier and collects them as they bounce off. (It is

ments at different places on the ice and listened for the sound of the explosions echoing off the bedrock. By measuring how long it took for the vibrations to travel from the explosion down to the bedrock and back, they could calculate the depth to the bedrock or the thickness of the ice. With enough measurements, it's possible to make a map of a glacier's underside.

Ground-penetrating radar is a similar way to map the glacier bed. The radar echoes off the bedrock, revealing an image of the bottom of the glacier.

You can also image a glacier bed by flying over it in a plane equipped with an instrument that measures gravity, or the force that attracts two objects to each other. The gravitational pull over a particular point on a glacier depends on how thick the ice is. The strength of the gravitational pull depends on

This radar image shows a large ice field in the Andes along the western coast of South America. The outlet glaciers are the brightly colored yellow lobes that terminate at calving fronts into the dark waters of lakes and fjords.

how massive the objects are and how close they are. Ice is not as massive as rock, so it doesn't pull as hard. The thicker the ice is, the weaker the gravity is.

It is also possible to visit the actual base of a glacier. People have dived under the Antarctic ice shelves. Some glaciers have natural tunnels and caves that you can walk into. At 650 feet (about 200 m) deep, the base of the Svartisen Ice Cap in Norway has several human-made tunnels and even a laboratory. Another way to find out what goes on at the bottom of a glacier is to study the sediments and landscapes it leaves behind.

An explorer stands in an ice cave formed under the Muir Glacier at Alaska's Glacier Bay National Park.

Glacier National Park in Montana is a landscape left behind by glaciers.

Chapter Four

Landscapes Left Behind

When you think of New York City, you probably don't think of a layer of ice so thick it would cover the Empire State Building. But if it weren't for the last glacial period, called the **Ice Age,** New York's landscapes—its rocks, rivers, streets, and buildings—would be completely different today. In fact, a lot of New York City wouldn't even exist.

Eighteen thousand years ago, ice covered three times as much land as it does today. Ice sheets in Canada, Europe, and

Ice Ages

Since it formed 4.5 billion years ago, Earth has gone through at least five long ice ages. The last one began about 4 million years ago. During this ice age, glaciers have advanced and retreated more than thirty times. The last time the glaciers advanced is known as the Ice Age.

Asia advanced across the continents, crushing forests, plowing up the soil, filing down the bedrock, and carrying billions of tons of rock from one place to another. When they retreated, they left landscapes completely transformed.

Scouring Out the Glacier Bed

Even the most solid rock has cracks in it. Water trickles down into the cracks and then freezes. Since water expands when it freezes, it widens the cracks, creating even more cracks. Eventually, this freezing and thawing in the cracks helps break pieces off the bedrock.

Ice is softer than most rocks, so it can't erode very efficiently on its own. But as the ice slides along the glacier bed,

A diagram of a glacial system shows how rocks scour out the glacier bed.

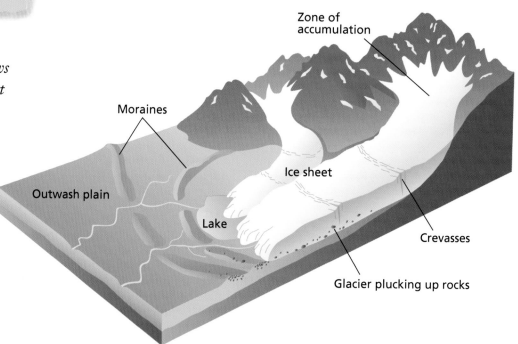

40

it picks up loose rocks and plucks up pieces of the bedrock. These rocks then get embedded in the base of the glacier. As the ice moves, the rocks scrape along the glacier bed, prying up other rocks and filing down the bed. This process makes the valley deeper and deeper.

Over thousands of years, thousands of miles of ice and rock scour out the glacier bed. What was once a winding, narrow, V-shaped stream valley can become a straight, wide, U-shaped valley. The top of the stream becomes a rounded, amphitheater-shaped cirque. Angular rocky outcroppings become streamlined hills. A small hollow becomes a deep, wide basin. Land that was once covered in a thick layer of soil is scraped clean, revealing polished and grooved bedrock.

Depositing Sediments

Glaciers build up the land as well as carve it out. The rocks that they erode in one place are eventually dumped somewhere else. **Glacial drift** is the collection of boulders, rocks,

Understanding Glaciers

The sediments that glaciers leave behind are called drift because people originally thought they were sediments that drifted with Noah's Flood. Until the late 1700s, scientists didn't know that glaciers moved and could change Earth's surface so dramatically. When a few scientists came to the conclusion that huge glaciers had carved much of the landscapes in Great Britain and northern Europe, people thought they were crazy.

Loose rocks and gravel, or moraine, left by a glacier lie near the peak of Mount Baker in Washington.

pebbles, and dust that glaciers leave behind when they retreat. A whole different set of landforms are made of glacial drift.

When the terminus of a glacier retreats, it leaves a moraine, a curved ridge of boulders, gravel, and fine rock powder chaotically mixed together. This glacial till fills low areas. The gravel that once lined the bed of a subglacial stream becomes a snakelike ridge called an esker.

Glacial Rebound

Glaciers have another dramatic, and somewhat bizarre, effect on the land. Large masses of ice are so heavy that they actually weigh down Earth's **crust.** The crust is the solid, rocky outer layer of Earth. Although we think of it as being hard and rigid, it is actually quite flexible. The Greenland and Antarctic ice sheets have depressed the land so much that it is now below sea level.

Even stranger, when the ice sheets melt, the land bounces back up. Scientists call this process **glacial rebound.** Glacial rebound is happening right now, on all the land that was covered by thick ice sheets during the Ice Age.

Scientists can calculate rebound using satellites that measure changes in land elevation over time. Sweden and Finland are rebounding small fractions of an inch every year. Since the ice sheet there melted ten thousand years ago, the land has risen as much as about 325 feet (100 m), leaving former beaches far above the sea.

Glaciers on Mars

Earth may not be the only planet that has seen glaciers plow across the land. Many features on the surface of Mars look a lot like glacial landforms on Earth. Deep, wide valleys resemble glacial valleys in Antarctica. Streamlined hills and snaking ridges look like those of glaciers. Hundreds of millions of years ago, areas of Mars may have been covered in thick, slow-moving sheets of ice.

An iceberg is surrounded by melting sea ice in northwestern Greenland.

Chapter Five

Freezing, Melting, and Other Hazards

Between about 1940 and 1970, the average air temperature at Earth's surface dropped slightly. Scientists warned that if it continued, winters would get longer and ice sheets would slowly expand, burying farms, towns, and cities. There would be less food because the growing season would be shorter. In many places, crops wouldn't be able to grow at all.

An avalanche crashes through the Savoia Pass on the northwest side of K2 in the Karakoram Range in Pakistan.

People as well as wild plants and animals would have to find new places to live.

Scientists are not particularly worried about global cooling anymore. It seems that the interval of cooling was just a little blip.

Now we have something else to be concerned about: global warming. Overall, Earth's climate is getting warmer. Most scientists do not think that natural variability explains the warm temperatures. Glaciers cause trouble for humans mostly only when they melt. Even though glaciers melt slowly, the effects can be catastrophic. Avalanches bury villages. Floods sweep away farmland. Glaciers calve off into the sea, forming icebergs that make it hazardous for ships to sail.

Changes in Sea Level and Climate

One of the main things concerning scientists is a rise in sea level. If all the ice on Earth melted and flowed into the ocean, sea level would rise 235 feet (72 m). This means that New York, Los Angeles, London, Sydney, and almost every other city on a coast would be underwater.

Of course, it is unlikely that all the ice on Earth will melt in the near future. However, some of it is melting every day, and sea level is rising. If sea level rose just a couple of feet, many coastal villages and cities would be devastated.

Melting glaciers could even change the climate in some parts of the world. When ice sheets melt, cold, dense water pours into the ocean. The water doesn't just stick around near the ice sheet, it flows around the world. If enough melt-water pours into the oceans, it will almost certainly affect the ocean currents. How exactly it will affect them, no one is sure.

The "Little Ice Age"

Since the Ice Age ended about ten thousand years ago, the climate has been relatively warm. However, around 1300 in Europe, it began to get cool again. For the next five hundred years, Europe had cold, snowy winters and cool, rainy summers. Storms and floods ravaged the coasts. Glaciers grew quickly down the mountain valleys, trampling forests and burying farms. Crops couldn't handle the cold, and many people starved. The Little Ice Age ended in the mid-1800s, when it began to warm up again.

Right now, Great Britain has a very temperate climate because a warm ocean current called the Gulf Stream warms the air before it reaches the region. The meltwater could change the course of currents such as the Gulf Stream. Without the Gulf Stream, Britain and northern Europe would be much colder.

Glacial Outbursts

Glaciers can also be melted from below. On September 30, 1996, the Grimsvotn Volcano erupted beneath the Vatnajökull Ice Cap in Iceland. The searing hot lava melted millions of tons of ice. About a month later, there was so much water inside the glacier that it cracked. Water suddenly poured out of the glacier and down the valley. In just half an hour, the flood of water was 10 feet (3 m) high and 1,500 feet (450 m) across.

This erupting volcano under Iceland's Vatnajökull Ice Cap caused mass flooding in 1996.

The flood from the Vatnajökull Ice Cap lasted for about a day and a half. It carved a channel 130 feet (40 m) deep and 800 feet (250 m) across, and brought millions of tons of sediment to the sea. It ripped enormous icebergs off the ice cap and destroyed bridges, power lines, and a major road.

Because Iceland has a number of active volcanoes and a major ice cap, huge floods like these are common. Similar disasters have occurred on other ice-covered volcanoes.

Uses for Glacial Meltwater

Of course, glaciers and ice sheets are not all bad news. They have many positive qualities. First of all, runoff from glaciers provides water to many living things, including plants and animals. There are even bacteria that live nowhere else in the world but inside the ice in Antarctica.

Humans have many uses for glaciers as well. Today, many people rely on glacial meltwater to provide drinking water and to irrigate their crops. In the arid western part of China, 10 percent of the freshwater comes from glaciers in the Himalayas. Bottled-water companies make huge amounts of money selling glacial meltwater. Hydroelectric plants in Scandinavia use meltwater to create electricity.

Small floating fragments of sea or river ice are called brash ice. In some parts of the world, glacial meltwater is used for drinking water and irrigation.

Earth's Freshwater

Glaciers and ice sheets hold 75 percent of Earth's freshwater.

Some people speculate that in the future, towing icebergs from Antarctica and Greenland to drier parts of the world might make sense. Then they could use the glacier's meltwater for drinking and irrigation.

Glaciers for Science

Glaciers are useful to many different kinds of scientists. Meteorologists can study the layers of dust in the ice to figure out how the air circulates around Earth. Climatologists use the air bubbles trapped in the ice to determine what the climate was like in the past. Environmental scientists use ice cores to see how air quality has changed over time. Volcanologists can date ash layers in ice cores to figure out when eruptions occurred. Biologists study the microscopic life-

A scientist takes a core sample of ice in Antarctica. Ice cores provide important information in many fields of science.

forms that live in the ice and in the lakes under the ice to improve their understanding of how life works and how it has evolved on Earth. Geophysicists measure glacial rebound to calculate how flexible Earth's crust is. Physicists are building a laboratory inside the Antarctic Ice Sheet in order to study mysterious particles from space called neutrinos.

Archaeologists have also found glaciers useful. In 1991, Ötzi the Iceman, a 5,300-year-old mummy, melted out of the Similaun Glacier in the Alps. Archaeologists studying life during the Neolithic period (the New Stone Age) were ecstatic. The ice had preserved the man, his clothes, his weapons, and even his last meals.

The Future

There is still much to learn about glaciers. If we are lucky, scientists will learn so much that some of the information in this book will be out of date in just a few years. There are

In 2002, the Antarctic's Larsen B Ice Shelf collapsed and broke up, reigniting fears of global warming. The photographs show (clockwise from top left) four aspects of the collapse: the shelf breaking up, a rift in the ice sheet, a cascade of water from melting ice along the front of the shelf, and the new front edge of the shelf breaking up.

glaciers in remote parts of the world that have never been explored. There are new ways of exploring glaciers that no one has yet tried.

Scientists still have many questions to answer. How old is the Antarctic Ice Sheet? What do the sealed lakes beneath the ice contain? Are parts of Antarctica melting so quickly that it is in danger of disintegrating? When will the next ice age begin? What if Earth's climate keeps warming? Are there glaciers on other planets or moons? Were there great ice ages in the past that we don't know about yet? How, exactly, does glacier ice move? In one hundred years, will there be any glaciers left to study? One thing certainly won't change: glaciers are fascinating to study.

Timeline

ICE AGES

About 2.5 billion years ago	The first known great ice age takes place.
800 to 600 million years ago	The second great ice age takes place.
460 to 430 million years ago	The third great ice age takes place.
350 to 250 million years ago	The fourth great ice age takes place.
4 million years ago to present	The Ice Age—the fifth and most recent great ice age—takes place.
About 10,000 years ago	The last glacial period of the Ice Age ends.

Around 1300	The "Little Ice Age" begins.
Mid-1700s	Scientists begin studying glaciers.
Mid-1800s	The Little Ice Age ends; nearly every glacier on Earth begins retreating.
Early 1900s	Explorers discover the Antarctic ice sheets.
1966	Scientists coring into the Greenland Ice Sheet reach the bedrock.
1968	Scientists coring into Antarctic ice reach bedrock at 6,681 feet (2,037 m).
1991	Ötzi the Iceman, a 5,300-year-old mummy, melts out of the Similaun Glacier in the Alps on the Italian-Austrian border.
2002	The Kolka Glacier in the Caucasus Mountains of southern Russia collapses.
2004	Scientists finish drilling the longest ice core so far. The core, from the East Antarctic Ice Sheet, is 10,726 feet (3,270.2 m) long.
2005	Scientists announce that nearly 90 percent of the glaciers in the mountains of Antarctica are retreating.

Glossary

ablation zone—the area of a glacier where most of the ice is lost

accumulation zone—the area of a glacier where most of the ice accumulates, mostly through snowfall but also the freezing of liquid water, wind depositing snow, and avalanches

advance—to grow, as in a glacier

alpine glacier—a small body of ice found among the mountain peaks and ridges; valley glaciers and cirque glaciers are alpine glaciers

bed—the rock beneath the base of a glacier

bedrock—solid rock beneath loose rock, soil, and ice

calving—breaking off

continental glacier—a thick layer of ice that covers huge landmasses near Earth's polar regions

crevasse—a deep crack or fracture on the surface of a glacier

crust—the solid, rocky outer layer of Earth

erosion—the process of breaking apart rocks and moving them from one place to another

firn—ice granules that have been on the ground for at least a year, sometimes called névé

glacial drift—sediments left behind when a glacier retreats

glacial period—a time period when glaciers dominate the landscape, also called an ice age

glacial rebound—the bouncing back of land no longer depressed by the weight of ice sheets

glacier—a permanent mass of ice that flows under its own weight; kinds of glaciers include valley glaciers, ice caps, ice sheets, cirque glaciers, fjord glaciers, ice shelves, ice streams, and outlet glaciers

glacier ice—compact ice with little space between the grains

ice age—a span of time in Earth history, lasting tens to hundreds of millions of years, when ice sheets covered large portions of the land; also called a glacial period

Ice Age—the last glacial period, beginning about 70,000 years ago and ending about 10,000 years ago

ice core—a cylinder of ice extracted from a glacier with a hollow tube or a drill

meltwater—water from melting snow and ice

moraine—sediment that is carried and finally deposited by a glacier

moulin—a drainage hole worn in a glacier by meltwater trickling down from the surface

retreat—to shrink in area, as in a glacier

sediment—an accumulation of loose rock of any size

surge—to move quickly, as in a glacier

temperate zone—a region of the world with a mild climate

terminus—the end of a glacier, also called the nose or snout

To Find Out More

Books

Downs, Sandra. *Shaping the Earth: Erosion.* Brookfield, CT: Twenty-First Century Books, 2000.

Gallant, Roy A. *Glaciers.* Danbury, CT: Scholastic Library Publishing, 1999.

Gordon, John E. *Glaciers.* Stillwater, MN: Voyageur Press, 2001.

Videos and DVDs

Alan Alda in Scientific American Frontiers XIV: Hot Times in Alaska, PBS DVD Video, 2004.

Glaciers: Alaska's Rivers of Ice, U.S. Geological Survey (USGS) and Alpha DVD, 2003.

Organizations and Online Sites

U.S. National Park Service
http://www.nps.gov/
This site will give you information about national parks and seashores to visit in the United States to see glaciers or landscapes that have been carved by glaciers.

U.S. National Ice Core Laboratory
http://nicl.usgs.gov/index.html
This site provides information about the U.S. National Ice Core Laboratory, which stores and studies ice cores from the world's polar regions, as well as details about visiting the facility in Denver, Colorado.

The World Glacier Inventory
http://map.ngdc.noaa.gov/website/nsidc/glacier/viewer.htm
Run by the National Oceanic and Atmosphere Administration, this site supplies interactive maps of more than 67,000 glaciers around the world.

NSIDC's All About Glaciers

http://nsidc.org/glaciers/

Run by the National Snow and Ice Data Center, this site provides information about glaciers, a glacier glossary, a gallery of glacier photographs, and links to news reports about glaciers.

NASA's Earth Observatory

http://earthobservatory.nasa.gov

This site provides information about the National Aeronautics and Space Administration (NASA) as well as links to a wealth of NASA Web sites, including the Jet Propulsion Laboratory's images of Antarctica.

British Antarctic Survey

http://www.antarctica.ac.uk/

This site provides information about Antarctica's weather and wildlife, recent news stories, and frequently asked questions about the Antarctic.

About the Author

Margaret W. Carruthers is the author of a number of Earth and planetary science books, including *The Moon* and *Pioneers of Geology: Discovering Earth's Secrets*, both published by Franklin Watts. After receiving her bachelor of science degree in natural resources from the University of the South, she went on to the University of Massachusetts to study the surface of Mars. She then worked as a geologist and educator at the American Museum of Natural History in New York City. Carruthers has collected glacial lake sediments in Massachusetts, marveled at the glaciers on Mount Rainier, flown over the Greenland Ice Sheet, and relaxed in the shade of glacial erratics in Central Park. Carruthers lives in Baltimore, Maryland, with her husband, Richard Ash, and their shepherd dog, Sifa.